Splat the Cat
and the Late Library Book

Based on the bestselling books by Rob Scotton
Cover art by Rick Farley
Text by Cari Meister
Illustrations by Robert Eberz

An Imprint of HarperCollinsPublishers

For Treeske. Enjoy.

HarperFestival is an imprint of HarperCollins Publishers.

Splat the Cat and the Late Library Book
Copyright © 2016 by Rob Scotton
All rights reserved. Manufactured in China.
No part of this book may be used or reproduced in any manner whatsoever without written permission except in the case of brief
quotations embodied in critical articles and reviews. For information address HarperCollins Children's Books, a division of HarperCollins
Publishers, 195 Broadway, New York, NY 10007.
www.harpercollinschildrens.com
Library of Congress Control Number: 2015950989
ISBN 978-0-06-229429-6

15 16 17 18 19   SCP   10 9 8 7 6 5 4 3 2 1
❖
First Edition

Splat's mom noticed that Splat had a lot of books and toys and clothes he didn't use anymore.

"Time to go through your closet," she said. "We're going to donate the things you don't need anymore to kids who do."

Splat thought that was a great idea . . .
but his closet was so stuffed he was scared to open the door.

Because every time he did . . .

SPLAT!

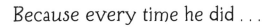

Splat went through his things and put them into piles.

"Look, Seymour! Remember this?" Splat asked.

"I think that shirt is too small," said Seymour.

"Oh, no, what's this? A library book—and it's way, way overdue!" said Splat.

TIGER TALES

BY BEN GALL

"How's it going up here?" asked Splat's dad.

"Great job, Splat!" he said, seeing all the piles. They decided to take the clothes to the local shelter. The toys would go to the children's hospital. And the books could go to the downtown library.

"Not the library!" Splat shouted.

"Why not? They're having a book drive today to get more books. People don't always return the ones they check out."

What am I going to do? worried Splat. His tail wiggled wildly. "The late fine will be ginormous!"

What will they do to me? Will they send me to jail?

"Hey, maybe I have enough money to pay the fine," Splat told Seymour. Splat grabbed his piggy bank and shook it hard.

He had only twenty-five cents.

"Time to go!" Splat's mom yelled. "Get your stuff together."
The family went to the shelter first. Splat tried to help his parents carry in the boxes of donations. Unfortunately, he might have tried a little too hard. . . .

DONATE

SPLAT!

DONATE

Next they went to the children's hospital. The kids there loved getting all those new toys!

The last stop was the library.
Splat was scared.

Mrs. Sardino the librarian met them at the door. "Thank you so much for your donation," she said, looking over all the boxes. "Splat, it looks like a lot of these books are yours."

Splat nodded.

"It must be hard to give away all those books. I know I hate to give up my books—even if I haven't read them in ages."

Splat started to sweat.

"I have a whole room in my house filled with books. Some of them I've had since I was your age. I should probably make a donation myself," she said with a laugh.

And that was all Splat could take. . . .

"I did it!" Splat confessed. "My library book is WAY overdue. I didn't mean to. I just loved the book so much I didn't want to return it. And I loved it so much I hid it in my closet. And then I forgot that I'd hid it. And it's like a million years overdue. And I'm really sorry. And if you're going to send me to jail or make me walk the plank, that's okay," Splat cried. "I deserve it!"

TIGER TALES
BY BEN GALL

FORMATION

BOOK DRIVE TODAY!

"Um, Splat," Mrs. Sardino said. "It's only a week overdue. You owe twenty-five cents."

"Seriously?" Splat said, reaching into his pocket.

"That's okay," said Mrs. Sardino, smiling. "This time I think we can let it go. Besides, your generous donation more than makes up for it."